For J+S+J, and for Janet
—**C. K.**

For the little girls told they're too loud, too quiet, too fiery, or too timid:
Know that you are special exactly as you are
—**E. M.**

Text copyright © 2024 by Carrie Kruck
Illustrations copyright © 2024 by Erika Meza

All rights reserved. Published by Disney 🔥 Hyperion, an imprint of Buena Vista Books, Inc.
No part of this book may be reproduced or transmitted in any form or by any means, electronic or mechanical, including photocopying, recording, or by any information storage and retrieval system, without written permission from the publisher. For information address Disney 🔥 Hyperion, 77 West 66th Street, New York, New York 10023.

First Edition, October 2024
10 9 8 7 6 5 4 3 2 1
FAC-025393-24129
Printed in China

This book is set in Futura/Linotype
Designed by Phil Buchanan
Illustrations created in mixed media

Library of Congress Control Number: 2023951255
ISBN 978-1-368-09497-9
Reinforced binding
Visit www.DisneyBooks.com

IGGY WHO BREATHES FIRE

Written by
CARRIE KRUCK

Illustrated by
ERIKA MEZA

Disney • HYPERION
Los Angeles   New York

Iggy was born with a spark.

Iggy turned three with a glow.

Her father fainted.

Her mother gasped. "Ignatia!"

"Whoa," said Iggy. "That felt good!"

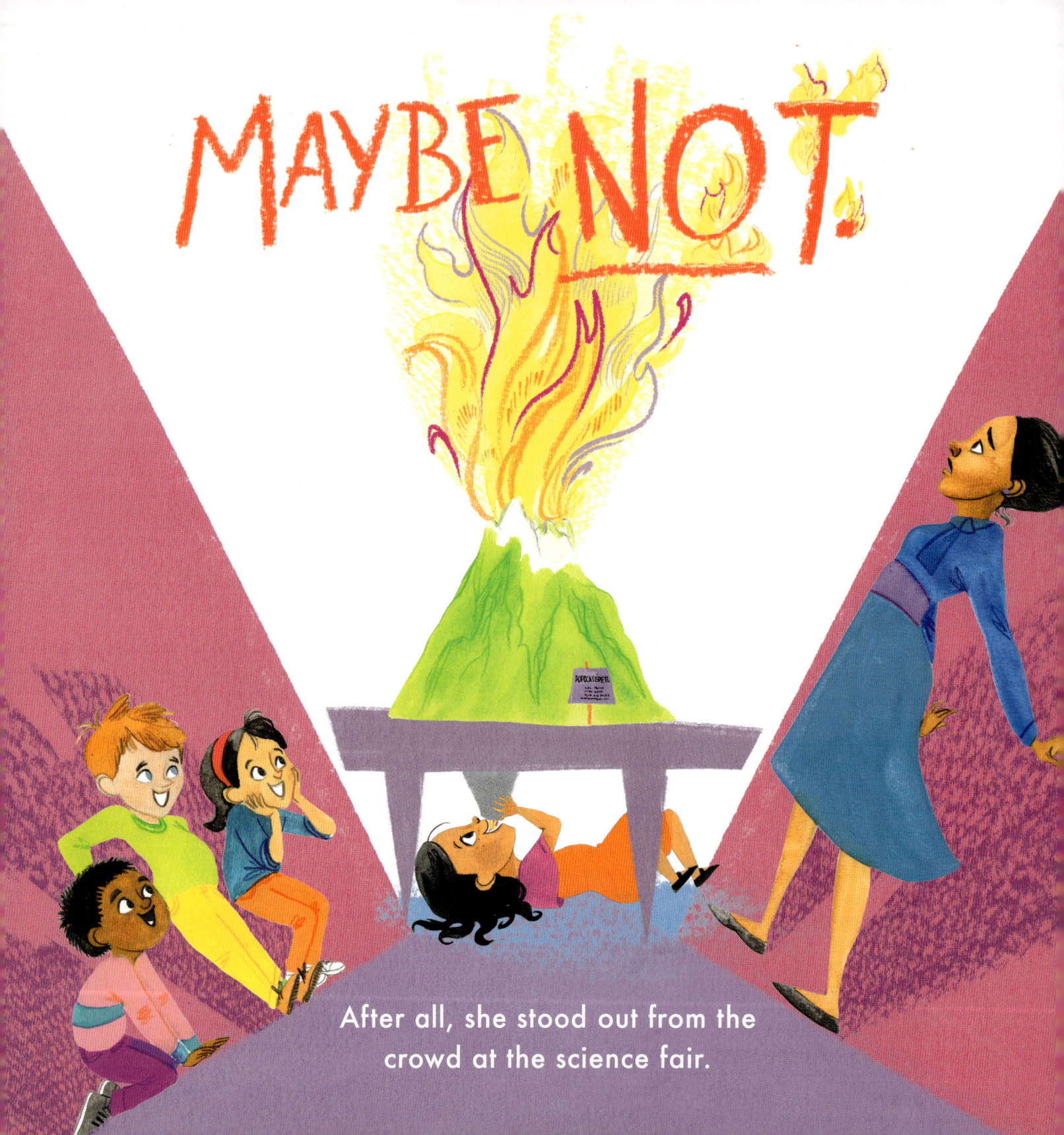

After all, she stood out from the crowd at the science fair.

Her Halloween costume was the talk of the town.

And who doesn't love a party with fire trucks?

Sure, sometimes fire-breathing could be . . . complicated.

But did Iggy want to stop?

"Maybe . . ." said Iggy.

Maybe . . .

"We have to do something," said her mother. Her father agreed.

But what?

Iggy's parents whispered to the librarian, but they found her advice alarming.

The fire chief thought ice cream might cool things down.
"Let's try triple chocolate next!" said Iggy.

The doctor just shrugged as Iggy tested her thermometers.
"That is one healthy set of lungs!"

"But . . . it's just . . . !" sputtered her father.
"What if . . . ?" worried her mother.

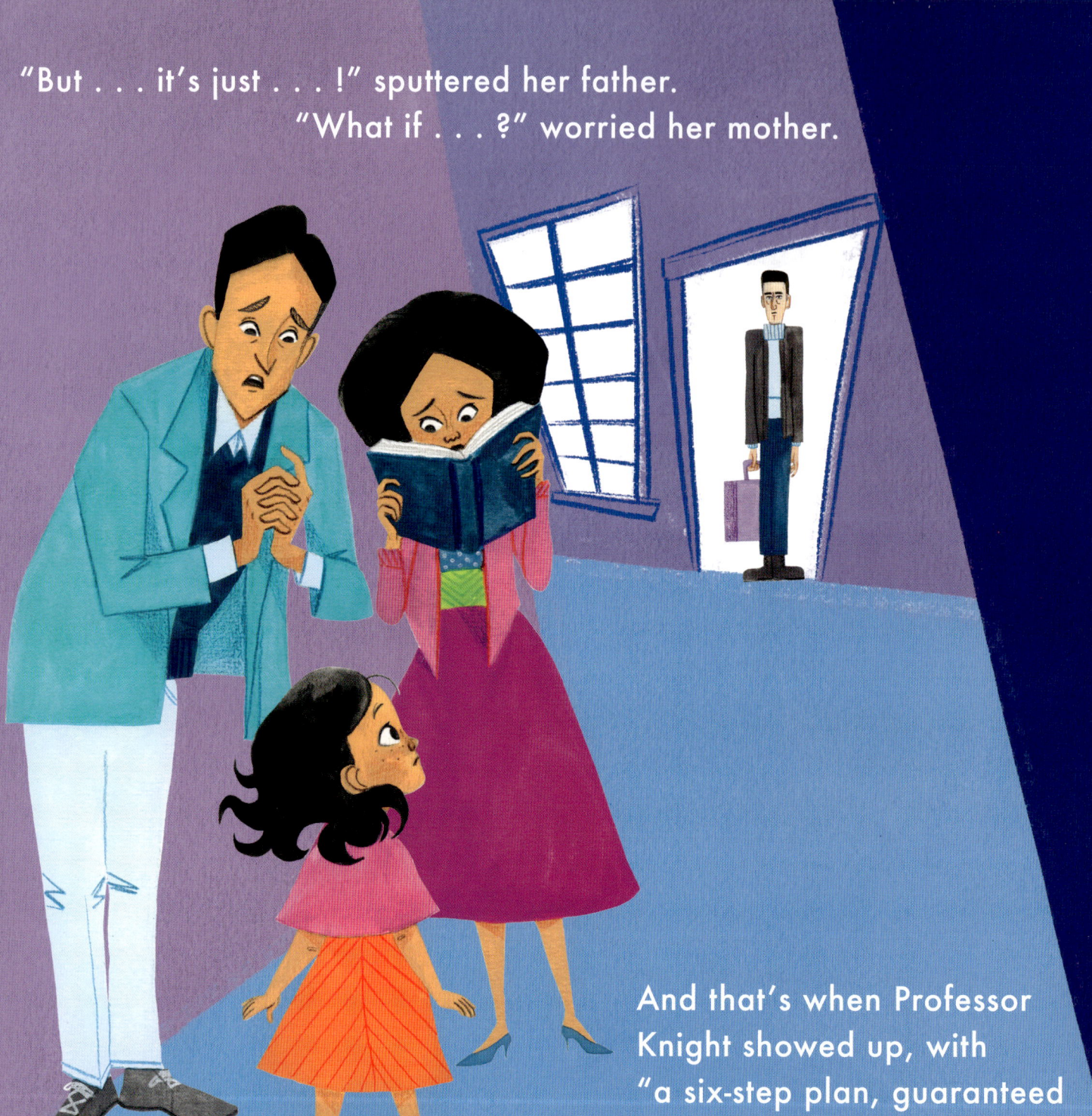

And that's when Professor Knight showed up, with "a six-step plan, guaranteed to help everyone feel better!"

"Step one," Professor Knight declared, "no spicy foods!" But salsa with no spice was just sad tomatoes.

"No sneezes! No hiccups!" Professor Knight blustered. But hot gasses always come out one way . . . or another.

"Excuse me!"

"No overheating!" Professor Knight fumed.
"No yelling!"
"No overexcitement!"

Maybe some people felt better when she held in her fire.

But Iggy?
She just couldn't hold it in any longer.

"I think it's time for an expert!" announced Iggy.

"Who?" asked her parents.

ME!

"At least, I will be soon," said Iggy.
"I just have to figure out a few things first."

Her father squeaked.
Her mother gulped.
But they looked at each other.
Then they looked at Iggy.

"Go on," they said.
"We trust you."

Iggy studied.

She practiced her aim.

(And always cleaned up her messes.)

"Staying hydrated is very important!" So was choosing the right kind of fuel.

FIRE NEEDS
OXYGEN
O = OXYGEN
H₂O = WATER

And soon . . .
her smile could light up a room.

Candles were a piece of cake.

Her marshmallows were perfectly roasted.

While snowballs didn't stand a chance.

But then the professor tried to call a meeting, to announce . . .

"Little girls DO NOT breathe fire!"

"Maybe you're right," said Iggy, "or maybe . . .

Iggy reached out her hand. "I'm Iggy, a girl who breathes fire. I also love spicy food, science, swimming, and marshmallows—and I always make extra to share."

Her mother beamed.
Her father glowed with pride.

Then Professor Knight took a bite of his marshmallow and said—

Who knows?
Iggy didn't wait around to find out what he thought,

because little girls who breathe fire?

They are very, very Busy.